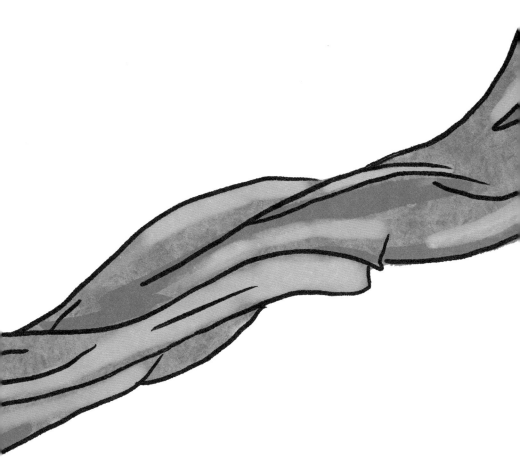

Rosie
to the
Rescue

The Story
of an Everyday
Superhero

Written by
Angela Kissel

Illustrated by
John Paul Snead

Printed in the United States of America

First Printing, 2020

Book Design by John Paul Snead

ISBN 978-1-7340479-3-6 (hc)

Published by Lola & Pear Publishing
www.LolaAndPear.com

This book is dedicated to my one and only Reese.
The little hippo pit bull who forever transformed
my heart and the hearts of many others.

- Angela

"Hi, little one. Hi, big one. You have a lot to say, don't you?! Come here, shy one, it's okay."

Gela arrived at one of the cages and saw a dog lying down completely wrapped in a blue blanket.

"Who is this?" Gela asked. "This is Rosie," a woman responded. "No one wants her."

"Why doesn't anyone want her?" Gela asked.

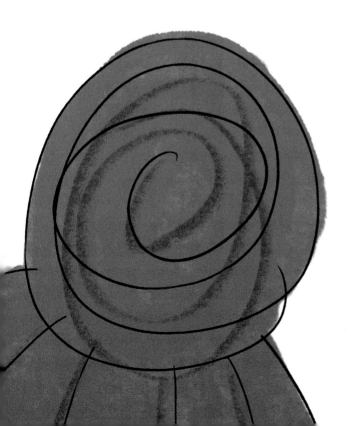

"Well, many dogs like Rosie are confused and scared about why they are in the shelter, and sometimes that makes people confused and scared about adopting them. So then really great dogs like Rosie never leave the shelter."

"But she looks so sweet!" Gela cried. "Who wouldn't want her?"

"Can I meet her?" Gela asked.

"Of course!" The woman replied.

While Gela was visiting with Rosie, she was thinking about what it might be like if she adopted Rosie. She knew that owning a dog was a BIG responsibility.

Dogs need walks, and food, and toys, and hugs, and... Gela knew she would have to pick up... dog poop! Eeeewwww!

But after looking at Rosie's sweet face, she knew it would be worth it. And most importantly, her mom said, "YES!"

Gela knelt down and looked at Rosie with her face in her hands. "How could no one want you? Do you want to come home with me?"

Gela took Rosie's excited, wagging tail to mean, "Yes!"

The first few days with Gela,
Rosie was very quiet.

She was sniffing, and sleeping,
and trying to get used to her
new home.

Gela was patient and loving as she welcomed Rosie into her new life.

But during Rosie's second week home, something special happened one night while she was sleeping. Rosie went to sleep as a shy shelter pup...

And woke up as
a superhero!

Gela couldn't believe it! The shelter accidentally gave her a superhero dog!

Gela and Rosie set out for the day to show off her new cape that they both thought was super.

"Wow, Rosie is so patient with my puppy!" Gela's neighbor Aleesa said. Gela excitedly replied, "She's super, isn't she?! Look at her cape!"

"I was thinking she's really kind," said Aleesa.

Rosie and Gela kept going.

CAPE?

Gela saw her friend Jack in the park.

"Look at her roll!" Jack said excitedly. "Yeah, she's super, isn't she?! Look at her cape!" Gela exclaimed.

"I was thinking she's really funny," replied Jack. Soon after, Jack joined Rosie and started rolling in the grass with her.

Gela decided it was time to take Rosie to the pet store. "Surely the pet professionals there will be able to tell she's a superhero," Gela thought to herself.

"She knew exactly where to go for her treats!" exclaimed the employee at the pet store. "I know, she's super, isn't she?" said Gela. "I was thinking she's really smart," said the employee.

Gela whispered back in a frustrated tone, "You mean she's suuuuuper smart."

Gela was beginning to think that no one found Rosie super except her.

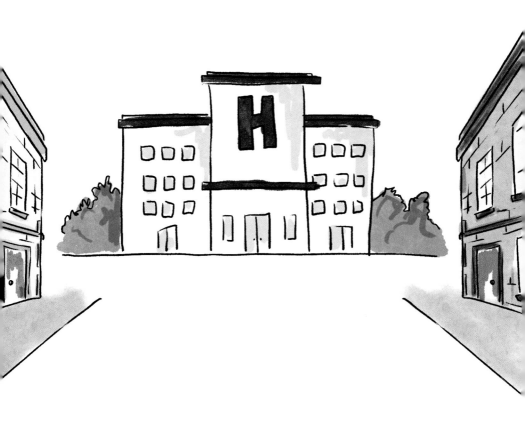

That evening, Rosie and Gela went to make new friends with people in the hospital.

"This is the first I've seen Mr. Thompson smile in a very long time. It's almost like Rosie knows to be gentle with him," the nurse stated.

Smiling to herself, Gela said, "Yeah, she's pretty..."

"Super!"

exclaimed Mr. Thompson.

"See! I knew she was a superhero. Just look at her cape!" shouted Gela.

"Cape?" Mr. Thompson asked.

"Umm, her superhero cape. That's why you called her super, isn't it? Because you saw her cape," Gela stated.

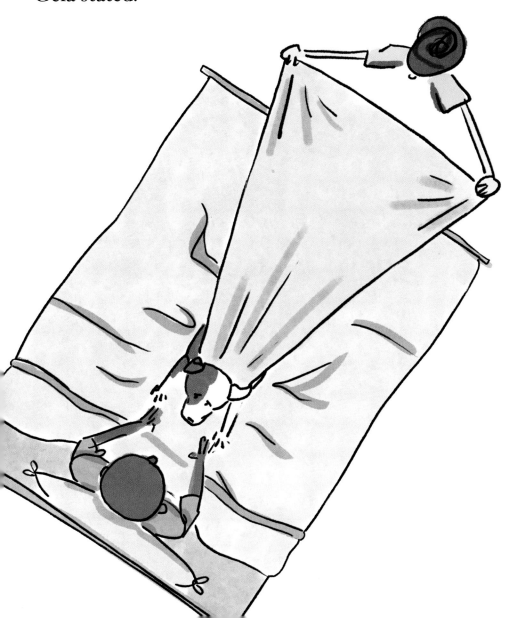

Mr. Thompson smiled, looked at Gela and said, "Well, of course she's a superhero; she's a dog."

"So all dogs are superheroes?" asked Gela.

"With a little love they are," Mr. Thompson replied.

Gela realized Rosie didn't become kind, playful, smart, and gentle because she woke up with a cape on.

She became those things because she finally knew what it felt like to wake up in a home that loved her.

And when dogs know they're loved, their humans can't help but see them for who they truly are:

SUPERHEROES.

"Goodnight, my little superhero.

I can't wait to love you again tomorrow."

The End

Lola and Pear Publishing gives 20% of the profit from our books to a chosen charity. Partnered with author Angela Kissel, the charity for *Rosie to the Rescue* is:

The Stand Up For Pits Foundation, Inc is a 501c3 nonprofit dedicated to educating, advocating and saving the lives of pit bull "type" dogs.

The SUFP Foundation has and continues to save countless lives nationwide through initiatives, front line rescue efforts and live events. To learn more and/or make a tax deductible donation, go to standupforpits.us

Stand Up For Pits Foundation, Inc.
www.standupforpits.us
ANGEL FOREVER

Angela Kissel is the proud mom of Rosie. When she's not walking around with Rosie through their Washington, D.C. neighborhood, she's most likely in search of her favorite food: pancakes. She believes that blessing others makes the world go round and that pit bulls are angels in disguise. Also, she's still picking up Rosie's poop, and Rosie's sweet face still makes all the ickiness worth it.

John Paul Snead is the Co-Founder and Creative Director at Lola & Pear Publishing. He is also a friend of Rosie's, whom she often refers to as "Uncle." They love going on walks together, and he even washes her cape sometimes. Even superheroes have laundry to do!

Hi! I'm Rosie! There are millions of superhero dogs waiting to be adopted right now in shelters, and many of them are pit bulls just like me!
Visit your local animal shelter or rescue organization to find out more!

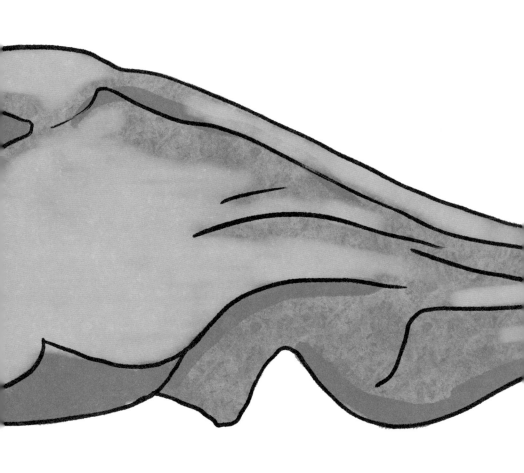